GREAT BEACH CAKE BAKE

6

BY JOJO SIWA

nickelodeon

AMULET BOOKS
NEW YORK

Cataloging-in-Publication Data has been applied for and may be obtained from the Library of Congress.

ISBN 978-1-4197-4597-3

Book design by Siobhan Gallagher

Printed and bound in the United States
10 9 8 7 6 5 4 3 2 1

Amulet Books are available at special discounts when purchased in quantity for premiums and promotions as well as fundraising or educational use. Special editions can also be created to specification. For details, contact specialsales@abramsbooks.com or the address below.

Amulet Books® is a registered trademark of Harry N. Abrams, Inc.

ABRAMS The Art of Books
195 Broadway, New York, NY 10007
abramsbooks.com

CONTENTS

CHAPTER 1

"**O**h my gosh, oh my gosh, oh my gosh!" squealed JoJo, clapping her hands. "I can't believe we get a beach vacation with Michelle Lee *and* we get to witness history in the making!"

"I can't believe you didn't remember to pack sunscreen," Grace chimed in, elbowing Kyra. "Lucky for you, this freckle queen"—Grace pointed at herself—"has plenty for us all." She reached into her bag and pulled out four large tubes of SPF 50, then lined them up on the dresser.

Kyra giggled. "Grace, you have enough sunscreen for an elephant," she told her friend. "What I can't believe is that we have a giant beach house all to ourselves. Party time!"

"*Almost* to yourselves," corrected Mrs. Lee, popping her head into the room JoJo was sharing with Grace and Kyra. "Don't forget about the mom on board!" The girls laughed. Michelle's mom was the coolest—they were all going to miss their own moms, but if JoJo had to pick, Michelle's was the next best thing. Well, besides Miley's mom, who was like JoJo's second mom. Actually, when she thought about it, they'd all lucked out in the mom department.

"How about a trip to the pier for ice cream in five?" Mrs. Lee asked. Kyra, Grace, and JoJo cheered. "Great!" Mrs. Lee said. "I'll let Miley and Michelle know." She ducked out of their room and disappeared into the hall and down a set of stairs to where Miley and Michelle were sharing their own room on the ground floor. It was going to be the best spring break ever—JoJo could feel it in her bones.

Five minutes later, everyone had gathered outside, next to the front door. Their beach house, which belonged to Michelle's family, had a name: the Saltwater Taffy! The name was written on a wooden sign near the driveway, and the house itself was bubble-gum pink and mint green. It looked nothing like the houses JoJo was used to seeing in Los Angeles. A wooden mermaid waved hello from above the front door, and a fisherman's net draped along one entire side of the house. In front, instead of regular grass, the entire yard was covered with little tufts of beach grass sprouting through piles of sand that had drifted over from the beach itself, which was just across the street. "Watch out for burrs," Mrs. Lee warned, since they were all wearing flip-flops.

"What's a burr?" Grace wanted to know. She sounded fascinated. JoJo perked up. In addition to being Grace's first-ever trip without her mom or dad, it was Grace's first-ever trip to the beach! Grace stared down at the yard through red, heart-shaped sunglasses. Behind them, her eyes were wide.

"This is a burr," explained Michelle. She knelt down and picked up the tiny, prickly ball between her thumb and forefinger. Michelle was wearing a polka-dotted one-piece bathing suit and denim cutoffs, and her long dark hair was wavy from the salt air. She stood and placed the burr in Grace's palm.

"It's like a tiny porcupine," squealed Kyra, poking the burr in Grace's hand. "Ouch!"

"I'm not sure I like burrs," Grace said, tossing it to the ground. "Mrs. Lee is right. I bet it would hurt to step on one!"

"It sure does," Michelle warned. "But if you're careful, you'll be okay!"

"I wonder what we'll learn about next," JoJo heard Grace whisper to Miley as the group started walking toward the pier. "I've never been to a place where houses have names." JoJo smiled. Grace loved learning, and there were so many great things to discover at the beach: beach glass and frozen custard and teeny tiny seashells and sandcastle building and boogie boarding. Grace was going to learn a lot that week—they all were! And best of all, they were going to watch two of their very best friends—Louis and Jacob, a dynamic baking duo—compete in the Great Beach Cake Bake, a baking contest televised nationally and filmed at the beach!

As they made their way to the pier, JoJo thought back to the way this new adventure had all come together. It had started with a text from Michelle, whom JoJo had become friends with through a dance workshop the year before. Michelle was a world-famous ice dancer! When Michelle invited JoJo to the beach house for spring break, well . . . how could she say no? And then a couple of weeks later, when JoJo was exploring social media, she had seen a casting call for a reality baking contest for kids . . . set in the same town where Michelle's beach house was! Louis and Jacob had entered as a team, and the showrunners went gaga for them. They had been accepted on the spot. After JoJo explained everything to Michelle, Michelle invited the entire group along to cheer on Jacob and Louis, who were staying in a beachfront hotel with all the show's other contestants. It was truly epic.

"Holy moly," Miley exclaimed when they reached the pier. "This is the coolest place I've ever seen!"

"Isn't it great?" Michelle asked, beaming. JoJo nodded—Miley was often dramatic, but it really was amazing. Besides the ice cream parlor with its giant revolving cone atop its roof, there were carnival games and photo booths and cute little souvenir shops.

"I want the pistachio! No, the strawberry," Miley said, scanning the buckets of flavors in the window. "No, make that rocky road!"

"You could get two scoops," Michelle's mom said. "My treat!"

"I'm going to get the golden albatross!" piped in a voice from behind them. JoJo and her friends whirled around.

"Jacob! Louis!" shouted JoJo. She ran over and tackle-hugged the boys. "Yay! I'm so glad to see you." It was the first time she'd seen the two since they'd arrived.

"Good to see you too, JoJo," Louis said, giving her a shy grin. Louis was new to the group, but he was warming up fast. They'd all met by accident during a school fund-raiser. JoJo and her friends had run a dog wash and puppy pageant, and Louis had baked the best homemade doggie treats around!

"C'mere, buddy," Jacob said to JoJo, slinging his arm around her shoulder. Then Miley, Kyra, and Grace ran over and squealed and hugged the boys.

"But where's your dad?" JoJo asked Louis.

"He's back at the hotel—it's only a few blocks away, so he said we could go get ice cream without him. He isn't feeling great,"

Louis explained. "But he'll meet us after ice cream."

"I hope he feels better soon," JoJo said. "Now come meet Michelle and her mom!" JoJo tugged on the sleeve of Louis's tee. "They're the best! And then we'll see about your golden . . . what was it?"

Louis laughed. "You'll see soon enough!" he told her.

Michelle lit up when JoJo walked over with Jacob and Louis in tow, as the other girls ordered at the counter. "This must be the famous baking duo," she said. "I've been SO excited to meet you both!"

"Same here," Louis told her. "I've never met a famous ice dancer!"

"Oh, pshhh," Michelle said with a modest wave of her hand. "But thank you." She brightened and turned to her mom. "Mom,

9

meet JoJo's friends who I told you about! They're going to be famous pastry chefs one day."

"Well, I can't wait to try your delicious treats!" Mrs. Lee said. "What would you two like for ice cream?"

Sure enough, Louis ordered the golden albatross. The waitress at the Lickety-Split laughed. "No one ever gets that," she said. JoJo could see why—it was enormous! It contained about ten scoops of ice cream piled high above a giant blondie and was covered in golden caramel sauce. Louis looked a little guilty for ordering such a big treat, and he thanked Mrs. Lee more than once. JoJo was willing to bet he didn't know what he was getting himself into!

"Trust me, I've got this," Louis told them as they settled on picnic benches with their

10

treats. But he looked doubtful, and the group laughed.

"If anyone can do it, it's you!" exclaimed Miley. For his part, Jacob had settled on soft serve dipped in strawberry glaze. He took one bite and nodded, satisfied.

"Excellent choice," he said, patting himself on the back.

"Oh, mine's good too!" said JoJo. She'd ordered a peanut-butter-fudge cone—it had peanut butter swirl in the bottom, chocolate ice cream in the middle, and peanut butter sauce on top. "This is delish! Thanks, Mrs. Lee."

"No problem," Michelle's mom said, smiling. "This week is all about fun, and the Lickety-Split is one of our favorite spots at the shore. We can't wait to introduce you kids to all the rest. Did you know the Lickety-Split is the official sponsor of the contest? See, there's a sign right there." She pointed at a colorful banner on the side of the ice cream shop. "It says they'll be giving away free scoops all day during the contest."

"No way! That's amazing!" JoJo exclaimed. "I'll be enjoying that for sure, along with the masterpiece cake you two will bake," she said, turning to Jacob and Louis.

Mrs. Lee nodded in agreement. "Boys, when exactly does your baking contest happen?"

"The contest is on Thursday—two whole days from now. We have loads of time to rest and enjoy the beach before we compete."

"You're old pros," JoJo teased, referring to another contest Jacob had won recently. That one had been live-streamed on YouTube. National TV was a whole other ballgame. "Are you going to practice first?"

"I don't think so," Jacob said with a shrug. "We bake together all the time! And we're pretty confident in our recipe."

"If you say so," JoJo said, a little worried. She'd known Jacob long enough to know that he was sometimes a little, well, *late*. Miley loved to tell the story of the day they'd met, when he was late to the first day of kindergarten. And usually when JoJo and the others came over for dessert, he answered the door in his apron. But, JoJo figured, that was why he had Louis—to balance him out. Maybe there was nothing at all to worry about.

"We're going to change into our swim trunks and learn how to boogie board after this!" Louis told them. "That is, if my dad's feeling up for it."

"Well, if it would help your dad, Louis, I'd be happy to keep an eye on you boys at the beach," Mrs. Lee offered. "The girls and I are headed that way in a few minutes."

"Thanks, Mrs. Lee," Jacob said. "That would be great. I'll text him to let him know."

"Are you sure about this, Jacob?" JoJo asked again.

"I am," Jacob said firmly. "Why be all stressed out before a contest when we could relax and have fun and show up fresh?"

"Good point!" Miley agreed. "You definitely want to be calm and energized for the competition."

"And prepared," JoJo reminded him.

Jacob and Louis both grinned. They didn't look nervous at all.

"JoJo, I'm always prepared," Jacob said. Then he arched his arm and tossed the remainder of his cone through the air toward the trash can.

The cone hit the can's rim and bounced off.

It landed on the ground with a *splat*.

JoJo looked at Miley, who was covering her smile with one hand. JoJo bit back a smile of her own and raised her eyebrows at her BFF. It was going to be a *very* interesting week.

CHAPTER 2

Jacob and Louis headed to the beach to grab a spot on the sand, while the girls headed back to grab their towels. A few minutes later, the kids were all settled on an array of colorful towels positioned under beach umbrellas. Mrs. Lee spread out her own towel a little farther down the sandy strip.

"This is so cool," Grace said. "Seriously the first grown-up vacation I've ever been on."

She tugged her wide-brimmed hat lower on her head and wrapped a towel around her shoulders and another one around her legs.

Kyra laughed. "Grace, you're all bundled up like it's winter! It's got to be hotter than a toaster oven under there."

"I burn easily!" Grace protested. "My big sister, Megan, says skin care is essential. She says you're never too young to start."

"But you're practically dripping in sunscreen," JoJo pointed out. "You must've put on a whole bottle. You know how crabby you can be when you're too hot," she teased.

Grace shrugged. "I'm not crabby. I'm happy as a clam," she told them, smiling.

"Did someone say . . . hermit crab?" Louis asked, running up to the girls. In his hand he held a shiny gray shell with red, creepy-crawly legs sticking out!

"AHHHHHH," shouted Kyra, jumping up

and scurrying away, just as Grace said, "No, Louis, we said clam! Happy as a *clam*!"

JoJo looked at Michelle, and Michelle looked at JoJo. Then the two dissolved in laughter.

"Louis, what have you got there?" Miley asked from behind her neon orange sunglasses. Just then, Jacob ran up too. In his hand was another hermit crab, bigger than the first!

"That matches your swim trunks," Grace pointed out. It was true—Jacob's trunks were covered in big, orange crabs. "Where did you get those?"

"A kid over there"—Jacob gestured toward the pier—"was selling them for a quarter. Mine's called Bro."

"*Bro?*" Michelle looked confused.

"I've always wanted a brother," Jacob explained.

"Jacob. That is a hermit crab. It cannot be your brother," JoJo said, laughing. "Did the person giving these crabs away say where he found them?"

"I think just by the pier," Louis told them. "Mine's called Blue Ribbon. Because that's what we're hoping to win on Thursday at this baking competition."

"I think you boys should put the crabs back where they came from," Miley suggested.

"I agree!" said JoJo. "Poor little crabs. They're a long way from home, in crab distance."

"We will," Louis said. "But first . . . a hermit crab race!" He handed Blue Ribbon to Grace, who wrinkled her nose. Then he stood up and dragged his hands through the sand like shovels. In the end, he made two long, parallel canals. When he was done, Louis placed Blue Ribbon at the end of one canal, blocking him to make sure he couldn't scurry away just yet. "Put Bro here," Louis said, gesturing toward the other canal. Jacob put his crab inside. Then Kyra put her fingers in her mouth and let out a piercing whistle.

Jacob and Louis let go of the crabs, who shimmied toward the finish line.

Bro, unfortunately, took a detour, scrambling up the side of the canal instead of focusing on the endgame.

"Bro!" shouted Jacob. "Left! No, right! Just a little more! You can do it!" But Bro had his own plans, and none of them included keeping his eye on the prize.

Blue Ribbon was victorious.

"Bro," Jacob scolded his little crab, who waved his claws furiously. "You really just needed to focus. It was like you didn't even care!"

"Winning isn't everything," JoJo told her friend. "Sometimes you have to lose in order to get better!"

"Well then, we'll see Bro in the Olympics next year," Miley joked. "Because he lost *bad*."

"Come on, Jacob," Louis told his friend. "Let's bring the crabs back to the pier and set them free. Then let's practice our recipe."

"Why would we practice when we've done it a million times, and on such a beautiful day?" Jacob asked, looking confused. "How often do we get a beach vacation?"

Louis shrugged. "Fair enough," he agreed. "I just think we should run through our list of ingredients to make sure everything's there. Everyone else in the hotel has been practicing in the hotel kitchen. Especially that girl Vera from Ohio." Louis shaded his eyes with his hand and looked back in the direction of the large, sprawling hotel on the beach where the contestants and their guardians were staying.

"Louis, we already double- and triple-checked when we were packing everything up back in Los Angeles," protested Jacob. "And the contest is two days away. We have plenty of time. Vera is just new to baking contests. She's probably nervous."

Louis tilted his head to the side, considering Jacob's words. "You're right," he agreed. "And you have more experience than I do with these big contests, Jacob. I trust you!"

"Cool," Jacob said, puffing out his chest. JoJo could tell he was enjoying Louis's compliment. "Let's put down these crabs and try out the boogie boards!"

"Sounds good. We're meeting my dad back at the hotel in an hour for lunch," Louis told him. "That leaves us plenty of time to boogie." He did a little shimmy, and they all laughed.

22

With that, the boys turned and headed back to the pier.

"They seem confident," Kyra said, digging her feet into the sand.

"Yes, but maybe *too* confident," Miley remarked. "I did some reading up on the contest online, and Vera from Ohio is supposed to be an amazing baker. She's from a line of Italian chefs who are famous for their homemade pastas, wedding soup, and cannoli!"

"Wedding soup? What's that? Soup you eat at weddings?" Michelle wanted to know.

"Nope. It's just a kind of Italian soup that has meatballs and greens and stuff," Miley explained. "Don't ask me why they call it that."

"That sounds delicious," Michelle exclaimed. "But I see your point about over-confidence. I've seen that happen before in my ice-dancing competitions. Sometimes people forget that hard work and preparation are a huge part of winning, no matter how much talent you have."

JoJo bit her bottom lip, worried. She trusted Jacob, but she also knew how distracting it could be to go on vacation to the beach. It was hard to stay focused on work when there were sandcastles to build and waves to ride.

"Guys," JoJo said, "I think we just have to support Jacob and Louis as best we can this week. What if we invite them to taste-test their cake on us?"

"Great idea, JoJo," exclaimed Michelle. "I'll ask my mom if we can invite them over for dinner tomorrow night. We can make the main course with my mom's help, and they can make the dessert."

"Guys . . . ," Grace said from her perch beneath a beach umbrella, where she was fully covered by her towel and hat. "I'm a little worried I'm getting a sunburn. Can we head back?"

JoJo and the others looked at each other and burst out laughing.

"Not before we jump in the water!" Kyra shouted. She grabbed Grace's hands and hoisted her up, causing the towel to drop off onto the sand. Grace squealed. "I'm afraid of the ocean!" she protested. "In theory, any-way." But she was smiling.

"Last one in's a rotten egg!" shouted Miley. She grabbed JoJo's and Michelle's hands, and the three ran for the water, with Grace and Kyra behind them.

CHAPTER 3

Later that night, the girls decided to go to a movie while the boys had dinner and played games at the hotel with their fellow baking competitors. Jacob texted JoJo, and after some conversation among the group, they decided that instead of dinner at the Lees' beach house the following day, they'd check out the hotel for high tea—another new experience for almost all of them.

Mrs. Lee walked them to the cineplex at eight, and they ordered popcorn. They'd chosen to see a film about a dog that befriended a dolphin—Grace's big sister had assured her they'd love it.

"My sister said this was kind of a tearjerker, but in a good way," Grace explained to them, tossing her wavy red hair over one shoulder. She was wearing denim cutoffs and a light sweater with a caticorn on it: a birthday gift from her sister, JoJo knew, and her favorite thing to wear. "I just wish she were here to see it with us!"

"Yeah, it really is too bad you're missing seeing her," JoJo told her friend, looping an arm around Grace's shoulders. Grace's sister was in college, and she was home on spring break that week. Grace had had trouble deciding whether to join her friends on vacation or stay at home to spend time with Megan.

"I wish there'd been some way to do it all," Grace said with a sigh. Then she brightened. "But Megan said it was important for me to experience new things. She's right! This is a good growing experience."

JoJo smiled down at her friend. JoJo and Miley were both used to traveling a lot due to their performance schedules—JoJo gave a ton of concerts all over the United States and sometimes even abroad. And Miley, a budding choreographer, was starting to travel for shows as well. And of course Michelle had been traveling all over the world since she was a little girl, for ice-dancing competitions. All three of them had attended loads of camps and workshops that required them to be away from their parents in unfamiliar places for days at a time. But for Grace and Kyra, being away from their families for a few days was a brand-new experience. Kyra seemed to be handling it fine so far, but Grace was still getting used to it. JoJo couldn't quite remember the first time she stayed somewhere without her mom, but she was sure she had felt much like Grace was feeling. Change wasn't easy!

After they got their popcorn, the kids filed into the movie theater and settled into their seats. As the lights began to dim, Miley leaned over and whispered in JoJo's ear.

"JoJo, I've been studying up online about the Great Beach Cake Bake, and every single one of the competitors is really incredible," she said quietly. "I'm worried that Jacob doesn't know what he's getting himself into."

"You might be right," JoJo whispered back. "But what can we do? We need to let Jacob and Louis figure this one out for themselves."

Miley nodded, but as she settled back into

her seat and the light from the screen flickered over her face, JoJo thought Miley looked worried. How could she make her friend smile? JoJo picked up a piece of popcorn from her bucket and flicked it at Miley. It hit her square on the cheek.

Miley giggled and flicked another piece back, but JoJo ducked—it just missed her. Before they could break into a full-on popcorn battle, the movie started. They turned back to the screen and settled in for the show. As JoJo watched Chunk the dog bond with Brahms the dolphin—it really *was* a happy-cry kind of movie!—she thought about how the most unexpected friendships could sometimes be the best. Only a couple of years ago she hadn't known Michelle, Kyra, Grace, or Louis at all! It had just been her, Jacob, and Miley. Kyra and Grace hadn't even really gotten along at first. And now they were all here together on a beach vacation. Life was full of exciting surprises.

"That was so, so good," Kyra gushed as the group left the theater an hour and a half later. "Grace, your sister was one hundred percent right!"

"I know!" Grace said, excited. "That part when Chunk jumped into the water off the speedboat and they swam side by side? So cute!"

"Want to FaceTime your sister and tell her how much we liked it?" Michelle suggested. JoJo smiled at Michelle, who totally got it— Michelle had a little sister herself, who was back home with their dad that week.

"Totally!" Grace exclaimed. She dialed Megan and held the phone up so every-one could fit in the screen. When Megan answered, Grace lit up. JoJo hadn't seen her so happy since they'd arrived.

"Hey, kiddo," Megan said. "What are you up to? It's late there! Hi, JoJo! Hi, Kyra! Hi, Miley!" she said, waving at the girls she knew.

"And this is Michelle," Grace said, angling the phone at Michelle, who smiled and waved. The kids chatted with Megan for a few minutes while Mrs. Lee observed with a little smile. When they were done, Grace blew her sister a kiss and tossed her phone in her bag, and the group started walking back to the Saltwater Taffy. Kyra and Miley skipped ahead, and Michelle hung back to talk with her mom, leaving Grace and JoJo in the middle.

"Are you glad you got to talk to Megan?" JoJo asked. She was missing her brother and parents herself, she realized. She'd have to shoot them a text later on.

"Yeah," Grace said. "But I don't know, JoJo. I just feel weird being way out here when I hardly ever get to see Megan, and she's back home. Not that I'm not having a great time with you guys," she said quickly, "but I guess I'm a little homesick." Grace crossed her arms over her chest and frowned a little. "I hope I made the right choice, coming here."

"I don't think there was a right or a wrong choice," JoJo told her. "It was a hard choice for sure—but you're here now, and we're going to have such a good time over the next few days. Think of all the new things you're going to learn and do!"

"It's true," Grace said, smiling. "Megan was the one who really encouraged me to come. She said going away to college has been a great learning experience for her, and she wants me not to be afraid of trying new things by myself."

"Grace," JoJo said, "you are one of the bravest people I know! You were new to the neighborhood not too long ago, and now look—you're part of an amazing group of friends, because you put yourself out there and weren't afraid. You're *already* doing all the things Megan wants you to do."

Grace bit her lower lip, looking thoughtful.

"You know what?" she said after a few seconds passed. "You're right. I *am* brave!"

"You just need to believe in yourself," JoJo told her. "You've got this."

Grace smiled from ear to ear, the first really big smile she'd given JoJo all day, and JoJo smiled back. "Now let's catch up with the others!" she said, pulling Grace ahead to join Kyra and Miley, who were just turning into the driveway of the beach house.

A few minutes later, they were all settled in their pajamas in the kitchen, having a mug of hot cocoa before bed. Kyra let out a giant yawn. "It's almost eleven, you guys! This is way past my bedtime!"

"It's vacation," cheered Michelle. "We can stay up as late as we want!"

"That's not *entirely* true," her mom said with a laugh. "Don't you girls want to enjoy the beach bright and early? I want you under the covers, lights out, in another half hour."

"No problem," JoJo said, running a palm across her tired eyes. "If I stay here much longer, I'll fall asleep on this table. Night, guys! You can find me here tomorrow when you come in for breakfast!"

Miley laughed. "I think you'll be comfier in a bed, JoJo," she told her friend. So the group rinsed their mugs, and Miley and Michelle headed to the bedroom on the ground floor while JoJo, Grace, and Kyra went upstairs. They all brushed their teeth, then snuggled under the covers. JoJo and Grace were sharing a queen-size bed, and Kyra had her own.

"Night, friends! Love you," Kyra said, as she shut off the bedside table lamp.

"Love you!" JoJo echoed. But Grace was quiet. Then, JoJo heard some quiet sniffles. At first in her sleep-haze, she thought the snuffles were coming from BowBow, JoJo's adorable pup. BowBow was always making funny little noises. But then JoJo remembered BowBow was back home with her mom in Los Angeles. So who could be making BowBow noises? JoJo wondered as she began to fade . . .

Then a sob jerked her awake.

"What?" JoJo sat up in bed and looked around. Next to her, Grace was wiping her eyes and sniffling. Kyra was snoring—clearly caught in a deep sleep—across the room.

"Sorry, JoJo," Grace said, breaking into a

fresh round of sobs. "I'm just really, really homesick."

JoJo rubbed her eyes and focused on her friend beside her.

"I'm so sorry, Gracie! I know it's hard," she said. "What can I do?"

"I don't think anything," Grace mumbled, hugging her threadbare stuffed tiger, Mr. Wrinkles, to her chest. "I don't think anything will fix this unless I'm home," she explained.

"Grace, if you still feel that way tomorrow, we'll tell Michelle's mom, and I bet we can arrange a different flight for you to go back home. But sometimes things look worse at night and better in the morning. I'm missing BowBow and my family a lot too. Sometimes when I'm missing them extra, I think about all the things we normally do at bedtime at home. Do you have a bedtime routine when Megan is home?"

"Usually Megan sleeps in my room, and we read some stories before bed," Grace explained.

"Well I'm no Megan," JoJo said, "but I *am* like another sister. Maybe we can read stories together for a few minutes."

JoJo could see Grace brighten in the moonlight. "Okay," she agreed. "I brought a really good book I've been reading. *The Phantom Tollbooth*."

"Phantom?" JoJo wrinkled her nose. "Is that scary? Do we really want to read that late at night?"

"It isn't scary," Grace said, laughing. "Gosh, JoJo. Are you a fraidy-cat?" she teased.

"*I'm* the fraidy-cat?" JoJo protested. "Really?" Then they looked at each other and burst out laughing.

"I'll get the book," Grace told her, climbing out of bed.

"Okay! We'll have to be quiet," said JoJo, motioning toward Kyra, who let out a big snore and rolled over.

"I think we're okay," Grace said, giggling again. She wiped a drying tear from her cheek. "I feel better already. Thanks, JoJo!"

A few minutes later, the two huddled over the novel with their phone flashlights on to light up the page. They took turns reading aloud, and JoJo did funny voices for the Humbug and Tock when it was her turn. Finally, JoJo couldn't keep her eyes open any longer.

"That was so fun," she said to Grace. "I'm glad we got to do something you do at home. Are you feeling a little better?"

"So much better," Grace told her. "Thanks, JoJo. I'm not sure I would have made it through tonight without you!"

"You would have," JoJo said. "But friends

make everything more fun. Hang on though, I have one rule, before we fall back asleep . . ."

"What's that?" Grace wanted to know.

"We have to make a new tradition to follow the old one. So your old one was reading books—now we're going to sing a song!"

"No fair! You're a professional!" Grace protested.

"Grace, this isn't about being good or bad, it's about having *fun*," JoJo told her. Then she began to scroll through her phone for ideas.

"Hmmm . . . not that," she said. "Not that . . ."

Then JoJo spotted it.

"Perfect!" she said.

"But what if I don't know the words?" Grace asked.

"You will, trust me," JoJo said, giggling. Then she put on the theme song to *Friends*, one of Grace's big sister's—and by extension, Grace's—favorite throwback shows.

"I'll be there for you . . . ," they whisper-sang, until JoJo couldn't help it and sang the lyrics at top volume, making Grace crack up.

"Guys, what's going on?" Kyra asked, rubbing her eyes. "Why are you awake?"

JoJo hopped over to her bed and belted out the chorus, and Kyra joined in, smiling. Then she threw a pillow at JoJo and yelled, "Go back to sleep!"

There was a light tap on the door—Mrs. Lee!

Sure enough, Mrs. Lee popped her head in the room. Her hair was rumpled in the back.

Oops.

"Girls, I'm so glad you're having fun," she said, "but it's way past midnight—get some sleep!"

"We're sorry, Mrs. Lee," Grace said. "I was

feeling homesick, and JoJo was just trying to cheer me up."

"Well I'm glad you're feeling better, Grace," Mrs. Lee said. "You girls are good friends to one another. Now . . ."

"GO TO SLEEP!" all three girls said, then doubled over with giggles. Mrs. Lee smiled and closed the door.

Five minutes later, the only chorus JoJo could hear was a chorus of snores.

And then her eyes grew heavy, and her pillow was so comfy, she began to drift off.

CHAPTER 4

"**W**akey, wakey," Miley sang, jumping on the bed smack in between JoJo and Grace. "You guys, the rest of us have been awake for hours!"

"Miley, get off!" JoJo grumbled. But she couldn't be mad at her very best friend. "What time is it?"

"It's almost ten-thirty," Grace said, checking her phone. "How did we sleep so late?"

"Because we were up so late!" JoJo said.

"You were?" Miley wanted to know. "Doing what? We fell asleep the second our heads hit the pillows!"

Grace looked at her hands, her freckled skin reddening a bit. "I—" she started.

"We were both super into a good book," JoJo explained. "It was hard to put it down." JoJo could tell Grace was a little embarrassed about being homesick. She didn't want her to feel put on the spot. Also, JoJo had a surprise cooking for Grace that she was afraid she'd give away if they kept talking about Grace's homesickness.

"Cool," Miley said. "You'll have to show me later. Now come down for breakfast! We have a big day ahead of us."

Downstairs, Mrs. Lee had prepped a huge breakfast of pancakes with strawberries, blueberries, and powdered sugar.

"So, girls. We have high tea at the hotel at

three o'clock. I spoke with Louis's dad, and it's apparently a chance for all the contestants to showcase their talents before the big baking competition. All the judges will be there too!"

"Whoa," breathed Miley. The judges were famous!

"So before we head over there, we'll have to get cleaned up and put on nice clothes," Mrs. Lee explained. "We have a few hours of fun before then, though. Would you rather boogie board or go play carnival games at the pier?"

"Games!" shouted Kyra.

"Pier!" said Miley.

"I'm fine with anything," Grace chimed in. "Although boogie boarding sounds a little scary."

"Boogie board!" said Michelle, laughing.

"Can we do it all?" suggested JoJo hopefully.

"We certainly can," Mrs. Lee said. "Just not all at once! Let's flip a coin."

She pulled a nickel from her purse. "Heads or tails?" she asked.

"Ummm . . . heads!" Miley exclaimed.

"Tails!" Kyra contributed.

"Okay, okay," said Mrs. Lee, holding up a hand. "How about heads is pier and tails is beach? Sound good?"

Everyone nodded. JoJo held her breath as Mrs. Lee tossed the coin in the air. The coin flew upward, spun a few times, and landed again in Mrs. Lee's outstretched palm. She flipped it onto the back of her other hand without looking, then lifted her palm.

"Heads!" shouted JoJo.

"Yippee," Grace cheered.

"I thought you were happy with anything?" Miley said to Grace, laughing.

"I am! But I've never been in a photo booth,

and now I will be!" shouted Grace. "This really is the week of new things!"

"This wasn't really a situation where we could go wrong," Mrs. Lee agreed. "Finish up your pancakes and then let's get moving! We have a day of fun ahead of us."

By the time they reached the pier, JoJo was ready for ice cream. Her mom had given her spending money for the trip, and so far she hadn't spent a dime, thanks to Mrs. Lee's generosity.

"Who wants some ice cream, on me?" JoJo asked the group.

"Thanks, JoJo, that's really sweet," said Mrs. Lee. "Just one scoop each, though—we need to save room for high tea!"

"Pistachio," Grace said.

"Black sesame," Miley requested.

"Rocky road," said Michelle.

And Kyra piped up with "peanut butter swirl."

JoJo went for the coconut cream pie flavor with graham cracker crumble.

Once they had their cones in hand, everyone began exploring the pier.

"I'm just going to sit on this bench over here with my book while you girls run around," Mrs. Lee told them, making herself comfortable. "Just make sure you don't leave the pier, and call me if there's a problem."

The girls agreed and scampered off. There were all kinds of games lined up along both sides of the pier—ring tosses, water guns, even a "go fish" for real live fish in a man-made stream! If you caught a fish, you got to keep it. And of course, there was the photo booth. It sat on one end of the pier with a dramatic red curtain stretching across the doorway.

"So cool," Grace said, as the group approached it. "Just look at all these props."

Right next to the booth sat a bin full of accessories—cardboard mustaches on sticks, giant plastic googly eyeglasses, and giant cardboard words saying things like SHAZAM and POW.

"Dibs on 'pow,'" Kyra exclaimed.

"Cute," Miley agreed, then giggled as she found a giant ZAP. "Should we do the photo booth now or later?"

"How about now?" JoJo suggested, wanting to make sure Grace was feeling great about the day. Grace tended to be quiet and didn't always speak up when she wanted to do something, and JoJo could tell she was practically hopping with excitement about the photo booth.

"Sure thing," Michelle agreed. "I have some of my cutest photos ever from this booth! I swear it's magical."

49

Grace beamed—she was already eagerly filtering through the bin of props. She pulled out a tennis racket, of all things, and waved it around. "I'm a tennis star for our first shoot," she informed them. The other girls dug around for their props and once everyone had something silly to hold on to, they all squeezed into the booth.

"Whenever I do this, I shout something random just before the photo is taken," Michelle explained once they were squished in—Miley and Kyra sat on JoJo's and Michelle's laps, and Grace crouched in front. "Just make a face that makes sense with what I say!"

"Okay!" Grace said, clapping her hands. "I'm going to push the button to start!"

JoJo held her cardboard top hat over her head. Grace pressed the red button beneath the screen and the clock started ticking.

Three . . . two . . . one . . .

"Ghostbusters!" shouted Michelle.

At first, JoJo didn't know how to react. Then she made her face into a "don't-mess-with-me" expression as Grace made a scared face and Miley held her phone to her ear to mimic "Who ya gonna call." Kyra looked confused, and Michelle was laughing too hard to do anything. Then the bulb flashed to take the photo, and the countdown started again.

Three . . . two . . . one . . .

"Stinky feet!" yelled Michelle, and they all pinched their noses or made grossed-out faces. The bulb flashed again.

Three . . . two . . . one . . .

"Megan's calling!" shouted Grace before Michelle could yell anything new. They all looked at Grace's phone, which was indeed lighting up.

"Hi, Meg," Grace said via FaceTime, and

they all waved to Grace's sister just as the flash went off for a third time.

The girls tumbled out of the photo booth, laughing. They'd done a few more rounds of photos so everyone could get a photo strip. "Christmas morning!" and "BowBow ate your homework" got the best reactions.

"That was super fun," JoJo told her friends. "I seriously can't wait to do it again. Great idea, Grace!" Grace blushed, bashful. JoJo was proud of her friend. Maybe she was still homesick, but she was really coming out of her shell and having fun.

"Ring toss next!" shouted Kyra.

The girls rounded the bend and began heading toward the ring toss booth when JoJo spotted a familiar face . . . times two.

"Jacob! Louis! What are you doing here?" Kyra exclaimed.

"Yeah," Miley said, tapping her foot.

"Shouldn't you two be prepping for high tea?"

Jacob turned in his stool in front of the shooting target booth, causing his water gun to miss its target.

"We're allowed to serve whatever we want at high tea," he explained. "We decided to do something simple so we could enjoy most of our day at the beach and on the pier." Louis nodded in agreement, although he was still focused on the race, aiming his plastic water pistol and furrowing his brows in concentration.

"We're saving our energy for tomorrow," Louis told them once he turned around. But his expression was doubtful.

"Or wasting it all on the pier!" Miley exclaimed. "Guys, isn't this your first chance to show the judges what you're made of? Are you sure you want to spend time playing games when you could be focusing on making a good first impression?"

JoJo could tell from Jacob's sour face that he wasn't enjoying being told what to do.

"Miley," he said, "we've got this, okay? It's just a baking contest. We're also here to have fun."

"Okay . . . ," Miley started. "But—"

JoJo grabbed her arm. "Ring toss?" she said to Miley, giving her a look and tugging her away from the water game. JoJo knew Miley was upset because she cared about Jacob, and JoJo was beginning to be a little bit worried herself. But worrying wouldn't help Jacob and Louis win—only Jacob and Louis could do that.

CHAPTER 5

One hour and three stuffed bears later, they all headed back to the Saltwater Taffy to get ready for high tea at the hotel. "Do we have to dress up?" Michelle asked her mom.

"Something a little nicer than bathing suits, for sure," Mrs. Lee said. "But how fancy you get is up to you."

JoJo pulled on her favorite rainbow-sequined skirt and a matching shirt. She finished the look off with a very glam bow and a pair of orange, sparkly sneakers. Grace and Miley each wore light sundresses—Grace's green and Miley's yellow—and Michelle wore a cute pink-and-white-striped romper. Kyra had on purple metallic leggings, a loose black tank top knotted at her waist, and high-top sneakers.

"Everyone looks fantastic," Michelle's mom commented when they gathered downstairs for the walk to the hotel. Mrs. Lee looked great too, JoJo thought—her short, dark hair was styled in a sleek bob, and she wore a gray linen sleeveless jump-suit with black sandals and a few gold bangles on her wrist.

"You look great too, Mom." Michelle gave her mom a giant hug. "But I don't know how we're going to eat all the treats at high tea—I'm still full from ice cream!"

"I told you!" her mom said, ruffling her hair. "It's okay, we're mostly going to support your friends. Snacks are optional."

JoJo had actually never been to high tea herself, but she thought it was something princesses did, so she was not entirely surprised to see that the hotel was very, very *fancy*.

"Whoa," Miley whispered as they walked into the lobby, which had soaring ceilings covered in gold. "Jacob's hit the big time!"

"He and Louis both!" JoJo said. It was true that the show the boys were in was about as big-time as you could get as a kid baker. "Next stop, Paris!" JoJo exclaimed. "Jacob's dream is to have a pastry shop right next to the Eiffel Tower!"

"I'd be okay with supporting them in France," Kyra chimed in. "I've never been."

"Me neither!" said Grace. "Well, obviously," she said, blushing.

"Not obviously, Grace," JoJo said. "You are very sophisticated."

"Thanks, JoJo," Grace replied.

"We all are!" said Michelle, twirling in circles in the hotel lobby.

"Sophisticated or not, what you need to be is well-behaved," Mrs. Lee warned. "Best behavior, please, Michelle." Michelle stopped twirling and rejoined the girls, but she winked at JoJo, who laughed. Michelle could be mischievous when she wanted to be.

"Now, who can tell us where to go?" Mrs. Lee wondered aloud. "This place is gigantic!"

As if on cue, a man in a dark blue suit approached them. He was wearing a gold nametag that read BRUCE.

"May I be of assistance?" he asked, twirling his mustache around his index finger. "Going to high tea, maybe?"

"We sure are," said Mrs. Lee. "We must have looked lost!"

"Lost, yes, but also very stylish," Bruce replied. "Do you have a reservation?"

As Mrs. Lee gave Bruce her information, the girls gazed at the very fancy lobby. The floor was all marble and there were velvet chairs and gold touches everywhere: gold vases, gold candlesticks, even a gold grand piano that was being played *that very minute* by a woman in a floor-length gown!

"I think this tea might be fancier than we thought," JoJo whispered to Miley, as the other girls gathered around the lady at the piano.

Miley nodded. "JoJo, it's always better to overprepare than underprepare," she said. "When do you think Jacob and Louis headed back?"

"Probably around when we did," JoJo said, feeling her stomach sink. She knew none of it was her responsibility, but she did not like to see her friends in a jam.

And JoJo couldn't have known it, but jam was *exactly* what Jacob and Louis were in, up to their elbows.

Mrs. Lee beckoned to the girls to follow her, and they all filed into a ballroom—an actual, real-life ballroom, as amazing as in *Cinderella*—and through a set of all-glass doors that led to a beautiful long deck that faced the ocean.

"Oh my," Grace said with a gasp. The view was incredible! Blue sky everywhere and crashing waves as far as the eye could see. JoJo had to agree—she'd been to a lot of places, but this was one of the prettiest. She clasped Grace's hand and moved toward their table, which was labeled with a sign in fancy writing that read, FRIENDS OF LOUIS AND JACOB.

The tables around them were starting to fill up, and JoJo noticed a lot of distinguished-looking grown-ups in attendance. She spotted Louis's dad across the deck and waved. He waved back cheerily. They had only met a handful of times, but JoJo thought Louis's dad was really nice.

JoJo was looking at the judges, whom she recognized from TV, when she spotted Jacob running frantically across the ballroom. She nudged Miley, who frowned and squinted—Jacob was barely visible behind the glass doors to the ballroom, but he was soon joined by Louis, who was waving his hands wildly. Their voices were loud, and JoJo was catching small pieces of their conversation through the open doors.

"I don't know!"

"Just redo—"

"—big disaster."

"Uh-oh," she said. The judges were starting to catch wind of the conversation, and they were peering through the glass doors to the ballroom at the contestants.

"I've got this," JoJo said. She pushed back from the table and walked quickly, but gracefully, into the ballroom.

"Oh, hi, JoJo," said Jacob, wearing a frown.

"We were just, ah, discussing strategy," said Louis, who looked uncomfortable.

"Everyone outside can hear you," JoJo told them. "Including the judges. Discuss strategy in the kitchen!" Louis blushed and looked at his shoes, and Jacob looked embarrassed.

"We didn't know everyone could hear," he told her.

"Of course you didn't. I think it's okay, if you hurry. Only a few people heard you guys. But what's going on?"

"Nothing," Jacob said. "We're fine."

"And what is that on your aprons?" JoJo asked. Then her eyes widened. In all the flurry, she had just noticed that Jacob's and Louis's aprons were both streaked with red and dotted with . . . seeds? She bent to take a closer look. "Is that . . . jam?!"

"We had a slight accident with the fruit filling on our three-layer tart," Louis explained. "It's all under control."

Outside, there was the sound of someone tapping a microphone.

"Gotta go," JoJo said. "Good luck!"

She blew her friends a kiss and ran back to her seat. Michelle and Miley both looked at her questioningly, but JoJo just shook her head.

"Welcome," said a voice from the front. It was the woman from the piano! Her beautiful gown sparkled in the sunlight. "It is our great pleasure to host the *very* important, *very* special welcome event for the Great Beach Cake Bake!"

"Very important?!" JoJo whispered.

"Very special?!" Miley whispered back. "Did Jacob and Louis not know this was a big deal?" The others at the table shared their worried expressions. The woman went on to introduce the judges and explain that she would be playing the harp while they all got a "sneak peek" of the "young prodigies' confections," which was fancy talk for "the amazing stuff Louis and Jacob were supposed to have baked." Then she called up the contestants for an introduction.

"This is Vera, short for Veronica," the hostess said, ushering a little girl with delicate features and wild blond hair to the front. "Vera is six years old but has already won many international baking competitions for her distinctive Italian flavors. She was also on the cover of *BB Magazine*—that's *Best Bakers Magazine*—last month for being a Top 10 Under 10. Last year, she completed an apprenticeship with Flavio Bonnelli, the famous chef. Tonight, you will be sampling Vera's mini tiramisus." Vera gave a humble wave as the crowd went wild.

"Whoa," Kyra said, leaning across the table. "She sounds pretty impressive. And only six! By the time she's our age, she'll have taken over the world, one cannoli at a time."

"Yep," Miley agreed. "I think Louis and Jacob are going to get more than they bargained for."

JoJo agreed. But she also thought a little competition was probably a good thing. She watched the judges smiling as Vera exited in her little chef's hat and apron. JoJo couldn't help but smile too. Vera was super cute! JoJo definitely had room for tiramisu.

Next was Gandalf, a twelve-year-old boy named after a character from a book.

"I go by Eric," he said when he was introduced. "That's my middle name."

Eric-slash-Gandalf was from Texas. His teatime treat was a bunch of very, very thin crepes—like thin pancakes—piled high, with cream between each layer.

Then came Winnie from Rhode Island— "Where my sister goes to school!" Grace exclaimed—who had made itty-bitty chocolate soufflés.

Then came Theo, followed by Valerie, then a duo act of Cameron and Izzie, then Akshara. Each of them had made something more elaborate and mouth-watering than the last.

Finally, Louis and Jacob were introduced.

"Louis and Jacob are from Los Angeles," the hostess in the green gown said. JoJo couldn't help but notice that Jacob's apron was still streaked with jam, and Louis looked flushed and out of breath. She wondered if they'd made a jam tart. "Jacob recently won the title of California Junior Master Pastry Chef, and Louis once started his own small business making homemade dog treats. For your enjoyment, the boys have made . . ." Here the hostess paused and squinted at the paper. "Peanut butter and jelly sandwiches?" Jacob looked at his shoes. "Well," said the hostess, forcing a smile, "I'm sure they'll be the best PB and Js you've ever tasted! Give it up for Jacob and Louis!" Everyone cheered, JoJo and her friends most of all. But JoJo couldn't help but notice that even Mrs. Lee looked confused.

A few minutes later, the lady in green

began to play a harp, and the waiters and waitresses began to pass out beautiful platters of the contestants' desserts along with tea sandwiches—little cucumber wedges and salmon triangles—and sweet treats like scones and petit fours. All of the contestants' treats were labeled with their names. When JoJo got to Vera's tiramisu, she practically gasped.

"This is amazing!" she said to her friends. "Have you guys tried it yet?"

"Best thing I've ever tasted," Grace confirmed.

"Best *ever*?" Kyra asked.

Grace nodded, her mouth too full to answer.

"I bet the PB and J will have something special about it," Michelle said hopefully. "Like, maybe it's a tiny cake and it's PB-and-J-flavored frosting in layers."

68

But when the tray containing Jacob and Louis's creation arrived, the girls' faces fell. It looked like an ordinary PB&J sandwich, cut into small triangles with the crusts trimmed off. JoJo reached for one hesitantly, still hoping there'd be some surprise. She took a nibble of the corner.

"It tastes like what my dad packs in my lunch," Grace observed. "Oh! I don't mean that to be mean. Shoot," she said.

"It's okay, Grace. It tastes like regular PB and J to me too," JoJo told her.

"Well," Mrs. Lee said, "maybe they're saving all their strength for the big contest tomorrow."

JoJo hoped so. She really did. But she saw Miley staring at something across the room, and she followed her gaze to the table of judges. They were all nibbling on the PB&Js and looking as though something was sour, not sweet. One of the judges looked confused, and another looked a little annoyed.

Uh-oh. Of all the contestants at high tea, Jacob and Louis had *not* made a good first impression!

That evening, Louis and Jacob decided to spend time at the hotel with the contestants again, but they FaceTimed JoJo and the others. They hadn't gotten a chance to catch up after high tea because all the contestants were formally meeting the judges and doing interviews. Being in the baking competition was a *very big deal*, JoJo was beginning to realize.

"We also need to go over our ingredients list, to make sure we're organized," Jacob explained. "Although I'm kind of tired. Maybe we'll just do that in the morning."

"Why not do it tonight?" JoJo suggested. "Then you'll sleep well and not have to worry about it."

"Good idea, JoJo," Jacob said. "You're right—there's some stiff competition. Akshara knows her way around a spatula! At least we don't have to worry about Vera, though."

"Why not?" Miley piped in from behind JoJo. "Her tiramisu was out of this world."

"Oh, she's so young and inexperienced. She's got talent, and she's been making practice cakes since we arrived, but there's no way she can stand up to the pressure once we're on the clock tomorrow."

"We'll see," Miley said. JoJo could tell her friend was fighting to keep her voice neutral. JoJo was a little bothered too. Vera might be the underdog, but she was mighty!

"What did you think of our PB and J?" Jacob

asked, his voice a little quieter. JoJo could tell he was embarrassed, but she had to be honest with her friend.

"We were a little surprised," she said carefully. "We thought maybe you'd make your famous brownies, or that tart you're so good at," she said, mentioning desserts Jacob had made for them in the past.

"Yeah, we planned to," he admitted. "But we ran out of time. And then we tried to throw together little lemon meringue pies, but it was a recipe we'd never tried before, and they didn't turn out. In the end, we borrowed bread from the hotel kitchen and used crunchy peanut butter from the hotel pantry. We did make the jam, though."

"The jam was great!" Kyra piped in. "I really loved it."

"I agree the jam is terrific," JoJo said

finally. "Totally delish. But you might have to work a little harder tomorrow to impress the judges. I've watched the show before, and they seem to favor cakes made entirely from scratch."

"That's what I said!" Louis called from somewhere behind Jacob. Jacob moved the phone so the girls could see Louis, who was playing a game on his Switch. "We're tossing our tried-and-true recipe and going fancy tomorrow to make up for today," he said, without looking up.

"Another new recipe?" JoJo asked.

"Go big or go home," Jacob said with a shrug. "We figure we've got to knock their socks off tomorrow."

"I guess so," Miley said doubtfully. "But won't that be harder for you?"

"We'll be okay," Jacob said.

"Just give yourselves plenty of time

to prepare," Grace contributed. Then she blushed. "Or, you know, don't listen to me. I've never even turned on an oven!"

"That was good advice," JoJo told her friend. Then she turned back to her phone. The screen now showed Jacob again. "Listen to Grace," she said. "Be prepared!"

"Stop worrying about us!" Jacob said—but he was smiling. "On second thought, thank you for worrying. It shows how much you care. But I promise we've got this." He let out a big yawn. "I'm going to bed. We've got to be up bright and early tomorrow. See you on the beach!"

"See you there!" JoJo said, then blew him a kiss.

"Bye, Jacob!" chorused the other girls. Then the screen went dark.

"What do you say we make signs to sup-port them?" Michelle suggested.

"I say hurray!" Grace cheered. JoJo grinned. Grace was getting more and more comfortable being herself and seemed to be thinking less and less about being away from home. But that wasn't going to stop JoJo from seeing through the trick she had up her sleeve . . .

CHAPTER 6

The next day—the day of the Great Beach Cake Bake—was a scorcher.

"Holy moly," Grace said, pulling on her polka-dotted two-piece bathing suit. "It doesn't seem natural to eat baked treats when we're going to be baking in the sun!"

"Seriously," Kyra agreed, slathering on lotion. "At least we don't have to be in a hot kitchen all day. I feel bad for those boys!"

"Oh, they're probably loving every second," JoJo said. She wiggled into her neon orange one-piece and pulled shorts on over it. "Jacob's always in his element when he's baking for an audience."

"It sure doesn't help his big head!" Miley exclaimed. She and Michelle had just popped into the bedroom, where the other girls were getting ready. Michelle had on a super cute, fringed white two-piece covered in a star pattern. Miley was wearing a hot pink one-piece that showed off the hot pink streaks in her long, wavy hair. Her favorite blue-and-pink headphones were looped around her neck.

"Miley—Jacob is our friend," JoJo reminded her. "Siwanatorz support one other."

"I know," Miley said with a sigh. "I'm sorry. I just miss the old Jacob."

Truthfully, JoJo missed the old Jacob too. The old Jacob never would have insulted the judges by serving PB&J at a very important event. The old Jacob used to taste-test every-thing for weeks (Miley, Grace, Kyra, and JoJo had been his guinea pigs a dozen times!) before taking it public. The old Jacob . . . well . . . he was a little less full of himself. Louis was new to the group, and JoJo had the feeling he was following Jacob's lead. If only they could get Jacob to be a good leader, JoJo just knew the day would turn out great.

"We have three hours to swim and soak in some sun before the judging starts," said Miley. "Let's eat breakfast super fast, then get going."

The kids scarfed down their cereal in five minutes flat, then headed out with Mrs. Lee, signs for the contest in hand.

"Whoa," Kyra breathed when they entered the public beach area. "It's totally different!"

It was true—aside from the sand and water and dozens of playing kids, the beach had been transformed. Lickety-Split signs were everywhere, and Lickety-Split vendors were doling out scoops of ice cream already even though it was only 9 A.M. There was also an enormous tent on a stage on the sand just below the hotel. Cameras and lighting equipment were being arranged alongside it. This, JoJo guessed, was where the presentation and judging would happen. And in fact, little Vera was already beginning to set up shop when JoJo and the others approached.

"Hi!" JoJo said with a smile. "I'm JoJo, and—"

"I know who you are!" Vera interrupted. "I'm a huge fan. And I saw you yesterday in the audience! I'm so excited to meet you!" JoJo laughed. Vera was practically jumping up and down, she was so excited. "I saw you live in concert a few months ago," she went on. "You were amazing!"

"Aw, thanks!" JoJo replied, laughing. "That's really sweet. But today we're here to cheer you on! And our friends Jacob and Louis, of course. These are my friends Kyra, Miley, Grace, and Michelle."

"Vera, your tiramisu was incredible," Grace said, brimming with enthusiasm. "I'm still thinking about it!"

"That's so nice," Vera told them. "I must've made it a hundred times! I'm glad it turned out."

"What kind of cake are you making today?" Miley wanted to know. "Don't you have to start baking?"

"It's a surprise," Vera told them. "But it's already finished. We were allowed to start baking at any point today after the kitchen opened at seven, and the rule was, we had to be finished in time for judging. So I got up early this morning. I just get really nervous about time, you know? Sometimes something goes wrong, and it can tack on a full hour to the process. Luckily everything went smoothly. So now I just have to decorate my booth!" She held up a bunch of glittery stars and hearts attached to a long piece of twine.

"Your banner is so cute!" JoJo exclaimed. "Do you need any help setting it up?" She eyed the sparkly banner, which was twice the size of Vera.

"No, no. You go enjoy the beach," Vera told them. "My mom and I have got this. She just ran inside to the bathroom, but she'll be back in a minute."

"So nice to meet you!" Grace gushed. "We can't wait to see your cake!"

Vera smiled and waved as they walked

over to the other contestants' booths, which were in varying stages of setup.

"Small but mighty," JoJo commented.

"Right?" Miley said. "So smart of her to prepare early so she can relax before the competition."

"Uh-oh," Kyra said. "Speaking of relaxed . . . guess who's *not* relaxed?" She pointed up toward the patio where they'd enjoyed their high tea the afternoon before. Jacob and Louis were standing up there, and they appeared to be having an argument. Like the day before, they both looked messy and splattered with every ingredient under the sun.

"This is not a good look," JoJo said. "I'll go talk to them."

"I'll come," Michelle offered.

"No . . . You all go back to our towels," JoJo said. "I don't want to draw more attention to them than necessary."

"Boys, amiright?" Kyra joked. "Let's go build a sandcastle!"

Miley and Michelle laughed, and the three of them turned and headed back to their spot in the sand thirty or so yards away. But Grace, looking worried, followed JoJo.

"I think you could use at least one person for backup," she explained.

JoJo nodded. "Thanks," she said. "From the sound of it, you might be right."

"—could have at least warned me we were out of sugar," Jacob snapped, not bothering to keep his voice low.

"You were supposed to stock the supplies!" Louis protested. Their words were clear as Grace and JoJo mounted the steps that led from the deck to the sand. Members of the crew were also going up and down the stairs, and JoJo wouldn't have been surprised if the judges were too.

"Guys!" she said. "Hey. It's us!"

Jacob and Louis stopped and turned toward the girls.

"Oh. Hi, Grace. Hi, JoJo," Louis said, looking embarrassed. "We were just . . . discussing some things."

"Discussing them loud enough for the whole beach to hear!" JoJo said. "Here, let's go inside the ballroom." Jacob scowled and ran a hand through his hair, coating it with flour. JoJo bit her lip and tried not to laugh—it would have only made him more angry!

"Tell me what's going on," she said, once the boys were seated at a table in the empty room.

"Jacob forgot to stock our supplies," Louis said, just as Jacob said, "Louis neglected to tell me we were out of sugar."

"Okay, so we'll get some sugar," Grace said. "There's a store just down the road."

"You don't understand," Jacob told them, his voice full of panic. "We were out of sugar, so I thought the salt was sugar. I poured an entire cup of salt into the cake filling for two of the layers! It's practically crunchy, it's so salty!"

"Oh no," JoJo said. She suddenly felt very bad for both boys, who looked miserable.

"Is there time to bake another cake?"

Jacob shook his head. He looked near tears. "It would take another three hours," he told them. "Plus the time it takes to get new ingredients. We only have an hour and a half left. We're done for. Only one layer survived."

JoJo thought hard. But she came up empty. It was true that cakes just took a long time to bake and assemble. The baking alone would take around forty minutes, she estimated. Not counting the stirring of ingredients and making the filling and frosting it. The boys really were in trouble.

"Unless you can think of a simpler recipe to bake, lickety-split," mentioned Grace.

JoJo froze, turning to Grace. "What did you say?" she asked, getting excited.

Grace looked flustered. "I said they'd have to be quick," she told them.

"No! You said *lickety-split*!" JoJo exclaimed. "Louis, Jacob, is there anything in the rulebook that says you have to *bake* your cake? Like in an oven?"

"Well . . . that's generally how cakes are made," Louis pointed out.

"And it's the Great Beach Cake *Bake*," said Louis.

"Yes," JoJo said. "But is there anything in the rulebook that says you can't make an ice cream cake?"

Understanding dawned on Jacob's face.

Then he reached out and grabbed JoJo's face with both hands. "You're a genius!" he said to JoJo. "You too, Grace!" He let go of JoJo and wrapped Grace in a hug.

"I've got the rules right here," Louis said, his own voice growing more and more excited as he spoke. "And nothing in here says we have to use an oven! It just says, be creative with what you have, and finish in time for judging."

Jacob was already pacing. "Okay, we'll still make chocolate crumbles for the filling," he said. "And there are parts of our cake we can salvage. We can use the jam we made yesterday for jam swirl! But we'll need a lot of ice cream," he said, his forehead crinkling. "Is this possible? I'm not sure we'd have enough money to buy it, let alone time to get it."

"All the signs say unlimited scoops," Grace said. "They don't say we have to eat them! You guys, if we all team up to bring you scoops, you may have just enough time to make this thing."

"You're so right," Jacob said, clapping his hands. "Oh, you two are the best!"

CHAPTER 7

All five girls spent the next hour running between the kitchen where Louis and Jacob were prepping for the contest, to the little ice cream carts for scoop after scoop of free ice cream!

"Can't we just take the gallon?" Kyra asked in frustration during her eleventh scoop run.

"No can do," said the Lickety-Split employee with a rueful smile. "Believe me, I'd love to stop scooping—my arm is getting sore! But I need to serve everyone on this beach. And I am operating under strict instructions to serve one scoop at a time."

"Okay!" said Miley. "Thanks anyway!" Then, as they scurried away, "Just be glad it's unlimited, Kyra—we've collected enough ice cream to last a person the whole summer by now!"

JoJo laughed. It was not how she'd pictured spending their day at the beach. And a very tiny part of her was frustrated that Jacob and Louis hadn't been more prepared. If they had been, JoJo and the rest of the crew could be making sandcastles and splashing in the ocean. But, JoJo reasoned, this was what Siwanatorz—and friends—were for: lifting each other up when times were tough. She was proud of all her friends for being good, supportive friends . . . even though Jacob hadn't always been easy to deal with the past couple of days.

"What are you kids up to?" Mrs. Lee wanted to know, when they took a quick break for water and snacks. By then, Jacob and Louis had finished the bottom tier of the cake, which was chilling in the freezer temporarily. That was the trick of it—getting the ice cream inside fast enough for the boys to mix in their own special ingredients and pop it back in the freezer before it melted! So far, so good, though—only one more, smaller tier to go.

"We're helping a friend," Michelle told her mom. "But we want you to be surprised." Mrs. Lee nodded, seeming to understand.

"Well, whatever it is, I can't wait to see it," she told them.

"You will in about a half hour," Grace told her. "Oh my! A half hour? We'd better get back to work!" They fanned back out among all the Lickety-Split carts. JoJo hopped from

91

toe to toe—there was a line at her cart! When she finally got to the front, the friendly lady scooping ice cream gave her a few extra scoops and a wink.

"Can't wait to see what you're up to," she said, echoing what Mrs. Lee had said earlier.

Hmm, JoJo thought. *Maybe this could actually work!*

Finally the cake was done. JoJo, Miley, and the rest were hot, sweaty, and tired from all that running around. But they had to admit, it was glorious. Jacob and Louis had used their PB&J filling to make a yummy swirl, and they'd cut up chunks of the original cake—the tier that *hadn't* gotten ruined by salt—and mixed that in too. They'd filled one entire layer with a center of chocolate crunch. And they'd lined the entire thing with homemade chocolate wafers.

"I just brought these for us to snack on

this week," Jacob explained. "But they're sure coming in handy now!"

"It's beautiful," JoJo remarked. "And the judging and filming are starting in five minutes! Let's get this baby outside."

The ice cream cake was heavy, but the three of them managed to get it down the stairs and over to the tent, with the others clearing a path for them. The cake was so tall they could hardly see over it!

"We made you a banner, since you didn't have time," Grace told Jacob, after he, Louis, and JoJo had settled the cake in the center of the table. "My sister, Megan, is in art school—she taught me a few tricks. I borrowed the colored pencils you had at the booth already—I hope you don't mind."

"Grace, you're a genius!" Louis said. "Thanks so much. Our booth wouldn't look nearly so cool without it."

"You're the best, Grace," said Jacob, admiring her work. "I remember your incredible face painting back when we had our neighborhood block party, but this is even better! Megan may have taught you some things, but your talent is incredible all on its own." The banner included an illustration of Jacob's and Louis's faces, along with illustrations of sand crabs, beach umbrellas, cake slices, and ice cream. It was cheerful and cute and *perfect*.

"Thanks, Jacob," Grace said shyly. "I had a lot of fun drawing it."

"Uh-oh," Miley said. "Guys . . . I hope you get to go first because . . . this cake is *melting*." Sure enough, some of the chocolate wafers were beginning to slide off one side of the cake. Jacob spun it around so that side faced him. "It'll be fine," he assured them. "We're about to start!"

JoJo could tell he wasn't so sure, though—a

94

bead of sweat was forming on his forehead. Or maybe that was just the heat, and not nerves. It was really scorching outside! She and the others retreated from the table and went to find their seats in the sand to watch. Michelle ran back to grab her mom, and the group reassembled as a whole just in time for the judging to start. They held up their signs, which read GO JACOB AND LOUIS! and YOUR BAK- ING TAKES THE CAKE!

"And . . . action!" shouted a crew member. Then the cameras were rolling. All ten contestants stood in front of eight towering cakes. They were, JoJo had to admit, some of the most beautiful creations she'd ever seen. Unfortunately, the judges started with Eric. JoJo had been hoping they'd start with Louis and Jacob.

"Come on, come on," JoJo whispered, eye- ing the ice cream cake. Streams of melting ice cream were starting to form on the sides, making the cake a little less pretty. But it was still standing solid.

"I didn't know they were going to ask them so many questions before tasting the cakes," Miley commented in a low voice. "This is taking ages!"

Jacob kept a smile on his face while Eric was being interviewed, but his eyes kept flickering down to the cake. A large chunk of the top tier fell all the way down to the table, making a loud *plop*.

"What was that?" one of the judges asked. Then, seeing the cake, she said, "Well. That's interesting." She turned back to Eric with a frown.

By the time the judges were done with Eric's cake, JoJo's heart was thudding, and one entire side of the cake seemed to be sliding off.

"We've got to do something," she whispered to Miley.

"What can we do?" Miley whispered back. JoJo shrugged helplessly. They had already done everything they could.

Then JoJo felt a tap on her shoulder.

"Here! Use these!" Grace said, waving around a packet of disposable cups. "I found them in Mrs. Lee's cooler." JoJo looked at Grace, confused. What were a bunch of cups going to do to save the cake?

"Milkshake!" whispered Grace. Then JoJo got it. She grabbed the cups from Grace.

"You, my friend, are brilliant!" she said. Then she stood and snuck her way out of the seating section and pressed toward the front of the stage. She waited until the camera guy's back was turned, then snuck up the side of the stage and handed the cups to Jacob, who looked just as confused as she'd been a moment before. A couple of the contestants looked over, but the judges' eyes were trained on Vera, who was motioning toward her French cream puff cake, which had a long name JoJo couldn't pronounce. JoJo stealthily darted back off the stage before anyone important could notice.

Back on the sand, JoJo looked up at Jacob and Louis. Both of them seemed equally baffled about the cups. They looked over at JoJo, and she made a shaking motion with her hands. Now she really *was* drawing attention! When one judge looked her way, JoJo broke into dance moves, pretending the shaking was part of the choreography. Desperate, she mouthed *milkshake* at Jacob and Louis. Suddenly, Louis's eyes lit up and his forehead smoothed. He gave JoJo a thumbs-up. And none too soon! Because not only were the judges heading to Jacob's and Louis's table next, JoJo was also getting dragged away by security.

"I was just trying to help my friends," JoJo said.

"You're disrupting the show," a tough-looking lady in a bomber jacket told her.

"Cool jacket," JoJo said, offering the security lady a huge smile.

"Okay, okay," the lady said. "You can still watch, but you need to sit quietly. No more funny business!"

"No problem," JoJo told her. She plopped down on the sand right there, not even bothering to make her way back to the rest of her group.

"What have we here?" asked an older man with short, graying hair and a beard and a name tag that read RAUL—not that he needed any introduction; he was the main judge of one of the most famous baking shows on TV!

"A puddle?" JoJo cringed. Sure enough, the cake was full-on melting now, and shrinking rapidly as its layers formed puddles on the table. A woman with neon blue glasses and a wild blond pixie cut walked over to join him. Her name tag read MAUDE.

"What sort of cake is this?" she asked, peering closely.

"A . . . *shortcake?*" Jacob tried lamely. A few people in the crowd chuckled, but JoJo put her palm to her head. *Doof.* The cake was indeed short, though. Even the milkshake idea wouldn't work unless the boys were quick about it! Otherwise they'd just have some soggy, sticky sand at their feet.

"It's an ice cream cake shake," Louis said, squaring his shoulders confidently. "Looks like a cake . . . well, kind of. And goes down like a milkshake!" He took a serving spoon and ladled some of the drippy, sticky cake into a cup. Then he placed another cup over that one to seal the opening, and shook it. Finally, he removed the top cup and handed the blended creation to the judge. Catching on, Jacob did the same, handing his own milkshake to the older gentleman.

"What's better on a hot summer day?" Jacob said, grinning.

"How . . . innovative," commented Maude.

"Very," agreed Raul, looking like he meant it. His regular mustache was now coated with a milk mustache. The corners of his mouth twitched. "You're really onto something here, boys. Tell me—did you two make this delicious ice cream yourselves?"

Louis began to fidget, and Jacob's neck, ears, and cheeks reddened. "No, sir," Jacob finally said. "We made all the swirls, fillings, and toppings. But Lickety-Split can take credit for the ice cream itself."

Maude looked taken aback. She exchanged a glance with Raul. "We'll have to discuss this in the greenroom," she told them. "That's the room where we judges meet to determine the results. Let's move on to the next contestant."

"It was a nice effort," Raul said to the boys, just loud enough for JoJo to hear, before he moved on to Cameron and Izzie and their tiered pineapple upside-down cake.

Oh dear. JoJo suspected that for all their efforts, Jacob and Louis may have just experienced their first defeat.

But both boys straightened their shoulders and scooped milkshakes into the remaining cups, passing them out to the crowd until everyone had a cool, sweet treat. JoJo was proud of her friends. She could tell what they'd realized: Winning is sweet, but milkshakes (and losing gracefully) can sometimes be even sweeter.

CHAPTER 8

"**A**nd the winner of the grand prize is . . ."

All seven friends stood inside the ballroom with Mrs. Lee, awaiting the awards ceremony, which was also being televised as the dramatic conclusion to the baking contest. Louis and Jacob had definitely added to the drama! And so had Vera, the youngest contestant in the history of the show! Vera's cream puff tower had been a hit, but the other confections had also wowed the judges. However, rumors were swirling that Akshara's English rosewater cake with lavender frosting was the sure winner.

"The croquembouche, by Veronica!"

The crowd went wild as little Vera—the underdog—moved to the front of the room to receive her trophy, which was as tall as she was.

"Croaka-what?" asked Kyra over the noise of the cheers.

"I don't know! It's a French thing, I guess," JoJo said, laughing. Trust the littlest competitor to pick the biggest cake name.

Maude presented Vera with her trophy, then leaned toward the mic.

"Veronica, thank you for being such a humble and positive part of our show today. How did you decide to make one of the most difficult cakes there is?" Maude leaned the mic toward Vera, who stood on tiptoes to reach it.

"I wanted a challenge," she said. "Something people thought was too big for a little girl like me to make. When I saw the cream puff cake I thought, 'This is it!' So I practiced a lot for a year until I got it right."

"A *year?!*" Jacob exclaimed. "That's like one tenth of my life!"

"And one-sixth of hers," JoJo pointed out. She laughed and patted her friend on his shoulder. "Just think what you could do if you practiced like that!"

"Thank you, Vera!" said Maude, clapping heartily. Vera's mom walked her offstage by the hand, while Vera's dad carried the enormous trophy. "Now for our second-place prize."

Second place went to Akshara, who curtsied when she accepted her prize. JoJo could tell Jacob and Louis were feeling miserable by the time third place rolled around. Sure enough, the third-place trophy went to Theo for his ombré chocolate caramel cake with a liquid gold (caramel) filling.

Jacob hung his head. "I'm sorry for letting you down, Louis," he said.

"Don't be silly—we're a team. We both slacked off," Louis told him.

"You boys did the best you could in the end," Louis's dad reassured them. "And next time you'll be better prepared." The crowd started to file out of the room. JoJo had just turned to go when she heard Raul's voice in the mic.

"We'd like to present one last award," Raul said. "This is an unusual one—we don't typically give honorable mentions. But one team today had a slow start and came up with a very clever solution to a problem they didn't expect. Being a pastry chef means thinking on your feet—problems arise all the time. A-*rise*. Get it? Ha, ha." The crowd chuckled politely. Raul cleared his throat. "Anyway," he said, "I would like to present Jacob and Louis with an honorable mention for creativity for their ice cream cake shake."

Louis and Jacob, beaming, went to accept a pair of blue ribbons. The crowd went wild—after all, Louis and Jacob's cake shake had been a welcome treat on a hot day!

"I hope to see you boys again in the competition circuit," Raul told them.

"But next time, give it your all," Maude said. "Being a chef is hard work!"

"We know," Jacob said. "Or at least we do now! Thank you so much for the opportunity to compete."

Louis said thanks too and shook Raul's and Maude's hands. "We actually have our friends to thank for the idea," he admitted onstage. "Our friends are on vacation—but they gave up a whole day of fun in the sun to help us dream up ways to finish our cake. They're the ones who deserve this award, not us!"

Jacob and Louis waved the girls up to the stage. JoJo noticed that Grace looked practically white with fright—she wasn't used to having all eyes on her! JoJo would have liked to mention that Grace was the one who thought of the milkshakes—but she didn't want to make Grace even *more* nervous, so she decided to congratulate her privately later.

"Take a bow, kids!" said Maude, and all the friends bowed to the cheers of a roomful of milkshake-happy guests.

After all the guests left, Louis's dad approached them.

"Time to go, kiddos. We have an evening flight back home to catch."

"We're going to the airport too!" JoJo said, before she caught herself.

Miley gave her a funny look. "We are?" JoJo glanced at Mrs. Lee, who gave her a wink.

"I mean. Um. In a few more days," JoJo explained. She'd almost blown her secret! That was a close call.

"Okay, weirdo. See you back in L.A.!" Jacob said, hugging her tightly. "And thank you for everything."

"We're so lucky to have the best friends ever," Louis added. "Thanks for turning this day around, you guys."

"Travel safe!" shouted Miley, as Louis's dad escorted Louis and Jacob out of the room. Then she turned to JoJo. "What was *that* about?" she asked. "Is there something you're not telling us?"

"My lips are sealed," JoJo said, grinning at Mrs. Lee. Michelle's mom returned her smile. "But let's just say the next few days are going to be even better than the first few were."

"I hope you're right, JoJo!" said Grace, stretching her arms over her head and letting out a big yawn. "But all this excitement has made me sleepy. Do we have time for a nap?"

CHAPTER 9

After their nap, it was time for dinner.

"But first we have to pick up a friend of mine," Mrs. Lee told them after they'd piled into the SUV. "I hope you girls don't mind—I thought she could join us for dinner."

"No problem," JoJo said, hoping she didn't sound suspicious.

"Sure thing, Mom," said Michelle absently. Meanwhile, Kyra's stomach rumbled from the back.

"We won't be long," Mrs. Lee assured them, laughing. "I'm getting the message loud and clear, Kyra."

"Can I FaceTime Megan while we drive?" Grace wanted to know.

"You can call whomever you like," Mrs. Lee said.

Grace dialed her sister, letting it ring three times . . . then four . . . then five. Finally she hung up, looking disappointed.

"Hm," she said. "Maybe she's out with her high school friends. She spends a lot of time with them when she's home for visits."

"Don't worry, I'm sure you can catch her later," JoJo told her. "Meanwhile, let's Face-Time BowBow!"

"JoJo! Dogs don't have FaceTime," Kyra said, giggling.

"Wanna bet? Here, watch." JoJo dialed her mom, and it connected on the first ring.

But instead of her mom's face appearing on the screen, it was BowBow's! JoJo cracked up laughing. "See! I told you guys I could Face-Time with BowBow."

JoJo's mom laughed from behind the dog, and she lifted BowBow's paw to wave hello. "How are you girls?" she asked when she'd put BowBow down. "We miss you!"

"Miss you too, Mom! And I miss BowBow a ton! Tell her I can't wait to see her furry face in a couple of days!"

"Same here. Tell me everything," JoJo's mom said. "Did Jacob and Louis win?"

The girls exchanged looks, then proceeded to fill in JoJo's mom on the events of the day. All the girls were so caught up in the conversation that they didn't even notice where they were headed until the car slowed to a stop.

"We're here," Mrs. Lee called out. JoJo said a quick goodbye and hung up the phone.

"We're ... at an *airport?*" Miley asked, confused.

"Is your friend arriving by plane?" Kyra wanted to know.

"She is," said Mrs. Lee. "And she texted me that she landed, so she should be walking out the door any minute. Grace, help us look for her!"

Grace hadn't been paying attention, because she was trying—unsuccessfully—to FaceTime Megan again. "But how will I know what she looks like?" She looked up from her phone and peered out the window.

"I don't know ...," Mrs. Lee said, then trailed off. The other girls exchanged looks. It was clear they thought something fishy was going on. JoJo bit her lip to hold back her giggles.

"Ohmygosh. Is that? No. No way," Grace

breathed, squinting. "Oh my gosh!!!! NO WAY!" Then she unbuckled her seat belt and jumped out the car without Mrs. Lee even giving her permission. Luckily, they were parked against the sidewalk, so Grace didn't have to go far before she leapt on top of—and nearly tackled—a tall, willowy teenaged girl with hair a few shades darker than Grace's, who was walking toward them with a duffel bag slung over one shoulder.

"I hope Grace knows that girl," Michelle commented.

"It's her *sister*," JoJo said, laughing. "Don't you recognize her from FaceTime? It was a surprise!"

"Oh! I thought she looked familiar," Michelle exclaimed, looking sheepish. "D'oh!"

By then, Megan was sliding into the front

seat of the car and Grace was hopping back in the backseat.

Megan and Mrs. Lee exchanged hellos.

"Mrs. Lee, is Megan your 'friend' who's joining us?" Grace asked, her cheeks flushed.

"She is," Mrs. Lee said with a smile. "A very new friend! I just met her for the first time right now."

"Ohmygosh, ohmygosh," Grace said again. "This is the best surprise ever! Megan, how did this happen?"

"Well . . ." Megan hesitated. JoJo could tell she wasn't sure how much to say in front of the group. "JoJo texted me and said you were having a hard time, Gracie."

"Grace? What, you are?" Kyra exclaimed, as Miley said, "Grace has been having a *great* time!"

"She's right, you guys," Grace explained. "I've been homesick. I've been trying to

116

cover it up, but . . . well . . . JoJo knew. Thank you, JoJo!" She leaned across the seat to give JoJo a hug. "This is the absolute best surprise ever!"

"Grace, I get homesick too," Kyra said then. "You should have told us about it—we could have helped you."

"I guess I was too shy," Grace told them. "I wouldn't have even told JoJo if she hadn't caught me crying in the night. You know me, I'm just not as brave as the rest of you."

"Grace! That is *not true*," Miley said as Mrs. Lee started the engine and pulled away from the curb. "You saved the boys today! Without you, they wouldn't have had any cake to share at all! But because of your idea, the judges were impressed."

JoJo nodded. "So true, Grace. And think of all the stuff we've been doing that's new this week—the photo booth, swimming in the ocean—you've totally left your comfort zone in the dust, girl." JoJo really wanted her friend to see how brave she was—it was clear to everyone else but her.

Grace thought about it, chewing her bottom lip. Then she grinned.

"You know what?" she said. "You're right! Maybe I had one hard night, but I've been having so much fun the rest of the time. And even though I missed Megan, I stayed. I could have asked to leave."

"That's right, Gracie," Megan said. "And by the way, I missed you too! Missing people or your home doesn't make you a coward. It makes you a girl with a big heart. I'm just so glad to be here with you now to enjoy the next few days! Have you girls gone boogie boarding yet?"

"Nope. We were supposed to today, but . . ."

"Our plans sort of . . . melted."

All the girls dissolved in laughter.

"Tomorrow, then!" Megan cheered. "Thanks for having me, Mrs. Lee. There's nothing I love more than spending time with my little sister and her friends."

JoJo looked at Grace, who looked like she'd won the lottery—or the baking contest. It made JoJo so happy to see her friend feeling better. But at the same time, having Megan around was kind of making JoJo miss her brother . . . and her parents . . . and BowBow . . .

"JoJo, you okay?" Miley asked. "What are you thinking about?"

"Oh, just my family," JoJo told her. "I miss them a lot too."

"I'm your family," Miley reminded her, giving her BFF a hug.

"You sure are," JoJo said, hugging her back. "Home is where the heart is, am I right?"

The girls dug into their pizza at Leo's Famous with gusto. Just as they were finishing up, Michelle's cell phone rang.

"Hmm . . . a number I don't recognize," she said. "I think I'd better see who it is." She excused herself and walked to the other side of the room, where it was quieter. JoJo saw her say hello, and then she turned to face the other direction, so JoJo couldn't see if the call was good or bad. Then she heard a loud squeal.

Michelle came racing back to them. "Mom, guess what!" she shouted. She didn't even bother to sit back down. "I got the role!" She jumped up and down, squealing some more, until other customers were looking at them.

Mrs. Lee pushed back from the table and

jumped up to embrace Michelle. "Sweetie, that's so great!" she exclaimed. "That is fantastic news! I'm so proud of you!"

"What's happening?!" Kyra asked, when she could clearly wait no longer.

Michelle sat back down, her face flushed, and her mom sat beside her. "I auditioned for a pretty major ice-dancing role for a Holidays on Ice production," she told them. "It's just a few months away, and I got the part! I'm playing one of the leads!"

"It's like a play on ice," Mrs. Lee explained. "This one's based on the legend of the Snow Queen."

"Ohhh, that's one of my favorites," Grace said delightedly.

"It's in December . . . at a ski resort right next to a giant ice-skating rink!" Michelle exclaimed. "Hmm . . . I wonder if I'm allowed to bring friends . . ."

"WE'RE IN!" shouted Kyra, Miley, JoJo, and Grace. Then they dissolved into fits of giggles.

"Another trip, Grace? You sure you've got this?" Megan asked with a wink.

"Oh, I've got this," Grace replied. "I've *more than* got this. I'm Grace the Brave!"

"You girls are adorable," Mrs. Lee commented. "Let me take a photo to capture this moment. Megan, you too! Get in there." She pulled back from the table and took out her phone, clicking to the camera function.

"One . . . two . . . three . . . !"

"FAMILY!" shouted Michelle, and they all made happy faces as the camera clicked away.

More books available by JoJo Siwa!